Who said hippos can't hop?

HIPPO D. HOP

Rich Pulin
Illustrated by Scott Kish

Published 2021 by Andrea Fox Media
©Andrea Fox Media LTD 2021.

Written by Rich Pulin
Illustrations painted by Scott Kish
Graphics by Andrea Fox

andreafoxmedia.com

For my beautiful daughters, Brooke and Sarah...

I had no funds to buy a new bedtime story for my two
very little girls who were only 5 and 6 years old; so I
made one up! I wrote Hippo D. Hop for them. They are
all grown up now, and I hope you enjoy the story!

- Rich Pulin

Once upon a time, not so long ago, and not too far away, in a little place high up in the mountains, in a green and rainy forest, near a very long, wide, and beautiful stream, lived a happy herd of special hippopotamus'.

They could do something that no other hippos in the world could do...

There in the rainforest, a time would come in the young lives of every hippo, when all of a sudden he or she would begin to hop!

Now, Hippo D. Hop was just like all the other baby hippos. She was cute and cuddly, loved to smile and used all the words that baby hippos say, "goo-goo, ga-ga, ma-ma," and, "da-da."

Hippo D. Hop's mommy and daddy taught her to wash herself, brush her teeth, and say her prayers.

She, like all other baby
hippos, soon could walk,
talk, run, laugh and play.

When she was a little older, at school
down by the river, Hippo D. Hop
learned her ABC's, how to color,
build with blocks and, sing songs.

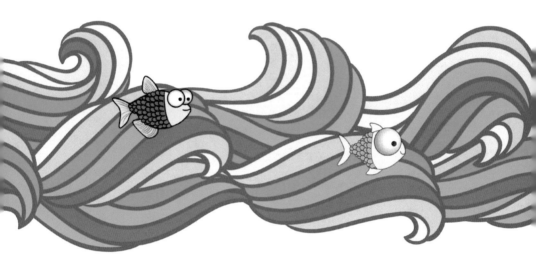

One day, while playing, in the misty magical forest, she noticed that her hippo friends were beginning to hop. "Hey! That really looks cool!" Thought Hippo D. Hop.

She tried hopping one
way, and the another.
She tried it this way and
then that way.

She tried hopping with one
foot and then with two.

Nothing worked! Then
Hippo D. Hop slowly
looked around. All of her
friends were watching her.

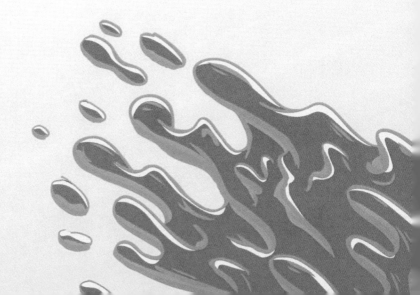

One of them called out, "Hey, Hippo D. Hop! A fine hopping hippo you are! You can't even hop! Hahahahahaha!" All her other hippo friends joined in and began to laugh at her too: "Hahahahahaha!"

That evening at dinner she said to her mommy
and daddy, "I feel very sad! All the other hippos
laughed at me today! What can I do?"

She looked over at her daddy with sad eyes.

"I don't want to be a hippo that can't hop!"
She began to sing...

Scan the QR code to listen to the song, or visit andreafoxmedia.com/HippoDHop

I Can't Hop

It's no use

I've been through it

I can't do it

I can't hop

All the other hippos, laugh and point at me

Won't some hippo have a little sympathy

For the lovable, cuddly, cute & adorable hippo

Who can't hop

Hippo D. Hop

The hippo who can't hop

The hippo who can't hop

Hippo D. Hop

Hippo D. Hop

Hippo D. Hop's daddy, a very wise hippo, said,
"Sweetheart, don't let those hippos bother
you. The same thing happened to your
mommy and I when we were little. Be patient,
all you need to do is keep trying."

He leaned over to her with a big smile.

"I know one day soon you will be able to hop too."
Her daddy's words made Hippo D. Hop feel a
little better but she didn't think she would ever
learn to hop. It was so hard!

The next day, Hippo D. Hop didn't feel like playing in the forest. She asked her mommy if it would be okay to visit her aunt, uncle and some cousins who lived close by. "Okay, my dear," said her mommy. "Please, be careful."

Hippo D. Hop waved goodbye to her mommy and walked down the road.

She was approaching the stream when all of a sudden she heard a strange sound. "Ribid, ribid, ribid, ribid."

She looked around and sitting on a rock in the water was a friendly, but strange looking green creature.

When she got closer, the creature jumped straight into the air and landed next to her on the ground.

Hippo D. Hop was startled and said, "EEK! What are you? You don't look like a hippo!"

"Me, ribid, a hippo? Ribid, ribid, hahahahaha; what makes you think that I'm a hippo?"

"Well, said Hippo D. Hop shyly, "you don't look like a hippo, but I saw you hop!"

"Hop, ribid, did you say hop? Hahahahaha, of course I can hop, ribid.

Everyone can hop. Can't they?"

Sadly, Hippo D. Hop shook her head, no and said. "Everyone, but ME!"

"You, ribid, you can't hop? Why, that's impossible!
Of course you can hop.

Let me show you how." He started to hop away
then stopped and turned around. "By the way,
ribid, my name's Freddy."

She smiled and said "Hi Freddy! My name's
Hippo D. Hop."

"Watch me, ribid" said Freddy and he began to hop.

He hopped over a branch of
the willow tree and into the stream.

He hopped out of the stream and over the bushes.

Freddy the frog was hopping all over the place.

"See how easy it is?" said Freddy to Hippo D. Hop.
"Now you try!"

Hippo D. Hop tried. She tried one way, then
another. She tried with one foot,
then with two. Nothing worked. Tears welled up in
her eyes. "I can't do it." She said,
sniffling.

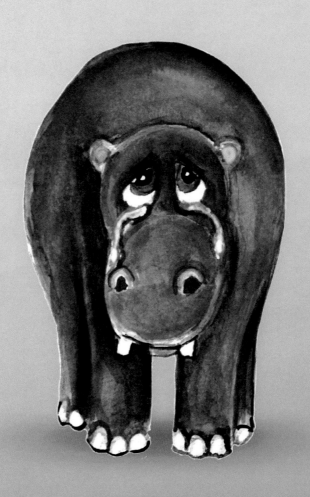

Hmmm, thought Freddy the frog. This is a bit unusual. Maybe she just needs a bit more practice and a few more friends to help her.

I know she can do it, if she just won't give up. "I have an idea," Freddy said. "Ribid, ribid, come with me, Hippo D. Hop."

So off they went, along the edge of the stream which flowed into a large pond.

At the pond, Hippo D. Hop saw two truly wonderful looking animals.

They had long back legs, and little front legs. They had big ears like a deer's and thick bushy tails. "Who are they, Freddy?" asked Hippo D. Hop.

"That is Ken, and his sister Kathy Kangaroo. They are marvelous hoppers.

Watch what they can do!"

Hippo D. Hop and Freddy the frog sat down under
an old elm tree and watched Ken and
his sister Kathy Kangaroo put on a wonderful show
of hopping.

They hopped over the flowers and over the bushes;
they hopped over a patch of toadstools and they
finished by hopping clear across the pond.

Freddy waved to the Kangaroos "Hello guys, I'd like you to meet my new friend, Hippo D. Hop, who comes from a hopping Hippopotamus family...

...but there is only one problem, Hippo D. Hop
CAN'T HOP!"

"Hi," said Ken as he bounded to a stop in front of Freddy the frog and Hippo D. Hop. "Hello," said Kathy as she too hopped over to them.

"Wait a minute, let me try and understand, you're a hopping hippopotamus, that can't HOP?!"

Hippo D. Hop sighed and put her head down.

The two kangaroos looked at each other deep in
thought wondering how they could help her.

"Oh, I've heard about you, a herd of hopping
hippos, that's wonderful!" said Ken with a smile.

"Well, that's the problem," sighed Hippo D. Hop. "I
can't hop, but when I watch you and Kathy it
makes me really feel like hopping!"

"You can." said Ken. "And you will," said Kathy.
"Let us help you."

So, as Freddy the frog looked on, Ken took
Hippo D. Hop by one hand and Kathy took
the other.

They showed her first one thing and then
another. They were nice to her and very,
very patient.

Hippo D. Hop started to hop all by herself.

First she hopped up the path, and then back down. She was even able to hop clear over the path!

Hippo D. Hop was so excited that she had almost forgotten where she was supposed to be going. "Oh, no! My aunt and uncle?" She cried. "They'll be looking for me, I've got to go!"

She started off down the path, then stopped and turned around. "Wait—why don't you all come with me! My family would love to meet my new friends who helped me learn to hop!"

They happily agreed.

Little did she know that all
kinds of animals had been
watching, and had seen her go
from a helpless, hop-less hippo
to Hippo D. Hop, hopping
hippopotamus!

The rabbits had seen her, and were so surprised by her hopping, they chattered excitedly to each other! Even Wally the Weasel was amazed.

The news spread quickly once the chattering squirrels found out and ran to tell Hippo D. Hop's mommy and daddy.

Her parents immediately left, taking the shortcut to be with the rest of the family when Hippo D. Hop and her new friends arrived.

As Hippo D. Hop hurried up the road to her aunt, uncle and cousins' home (hopping all the way, of course, and laughing), she could feel that something special was happening.

There was music in the air, and she could hear laughter. It sounded like a party. There were all kinds of delicious smells, too.

"That, ribid, sounds like music, ribid, ribid," exclaimed an excited Freddy the frog.

As they got close enough to see, Hippo D. Hop couldn't believe her eyes. There, under the big oak tree, were her mommy and daddy, along with her aunt, uncle and cousins. As a matter of fact, the whole hippopotamus family was there.

There were tables full of good things to eat. The band was playing and everyone was hopping and dancing and having a great time.

"There's Hippo D. Hop!" shouted one of her cousins. Everyone was looking at her, but this time they weren't laughing. They were smiling, clapping and cheering.

Hippo D. Hop went all around and hugged everyone! "Everybody, look, look!" Hippo D. Hop said excitedly.

And with that she started to hop and sing...

Scan the QR code to listen to the song, or
visit andreafoxmedia.com/HippoDHop

SCAN
ME

I Can Hop

I can Hop
I can Hop
I'm on top of the world
Everything's okay
I can Hop
I can Hop
I can Hippity Hop
It's such a happy day
It's fun being one of the hippity Hopping Hippos
It's neat and real sweet when your hopping with
all the hippos
I can Hop
I can Hop
Do a flippity flop
What a happy day
A very happy day
It's a happy day

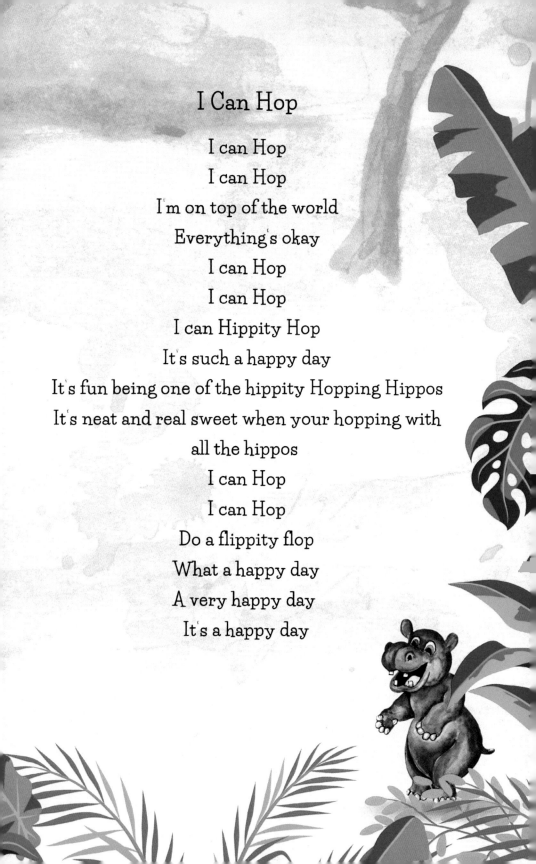

Hippo D. Hop hopped all over the
yard. She then hopped over the
table where her mommy, daddy,
uncle, aunt and cousins were
sitting.

She even hopped over the
musicians, who were playing the
most joyful music Hippo D. Hop
had ever heard.

Hippo D. Hop was so excited, because
she learned, that when she kept on
trying... She could do it!

And with that, she hopped, and hopped,
and hopped!

The Hippity-Hoppin End!

About the Author

The launch of Hippo D. Hop celebrates the 80th birthday of Rich Pulin, a jazz musician from Las Vegas, who beautifully wrote this delightful children's story for his young daughters a long time ago. As a single dad, he got tired of reading the same stories to his girls at bedtime and decided to write them one - all of their own.

Rich Pulin has, so far, had a glittering career as a trombone player and is the founder of The Rich Pulin Musical Family. He also wrote and recorded the two songs featured in the story - with stunning vocals performed by Brooke Pulin, Rich's eldest daughter. Some of the names Rich has worked with are among the greats; Billy Mitchel, Richard Harris, Joe Cocker and Lulu, to name but a few! He even had a European platinum selling song, 'Boogie Woogie Woman,' in 1974.

To celebrate 80 years on Earth, Rich is launching his autobiography, 'My Miraculous Musical Mission,' and a collection of his musical works called 'Seasons,' together with 'Hippo D. Hop.' Many happy returns Mr Pulin!

About the Artist

Scott Kish is an exciting artist who lives in Ontario, Canada. He has studied Kenesiology - the science of movement - at The Universty of Waterloo and has taken this interest into his art work.

Scott paints stunning watercolor paintings which show how people, animals and objects move with lines, splashes and dashes. Although, 'Hippo D. Hop' is a little different, as the creatures in the book are painted to look especially appealing to youngsters. We think you might agree, they are very cute!

Did you enjoy this book?

You can find out about more
books on this website:

andreafoxmedia.com/kids

Look out for other titles...

Made in the USA
Columbia, SC
17 October 2021